Poe-ish Tales Forevermore

A Mini-anthology

Contents

An Unkindness

by Vonnie Winslow Crist

"Graveyard soil would rather stay undisturbed," said Brig.

"Dig," responded Quentin. "It is easy money. With university expenses, we both need the funds to cover our bills. Besides, Baltimore is the ideal spot for *resurrectionists.*"

"I know."

"Look, the city has a large population, the climate is moderate, there are plenty of medical schools nearby willing to pay for cadavers," said Quentin.

"I said, I know." Brig clenched and unclenched the handle of his shovel several times before muttering, "But things beneath the ground don't want to be dug up."

"Blast it! We need to get the bodies to Danny-O tonight," Quentin reminded his friend. "His whiskey ships on a freight train pulling out of Baltimore day after tomorrow. So dig."

"It still gives me the creeps," replied Brig.

As if to punctuate the macabre nature of their enterprise, the twenty or more ravens who had been following Quentin for the last month landed atop several headstones and statues a few yards from the targeted grave. Their abrasive squawks seemed accusatory.

"I'll shoo away the birds if it makes you feel better," offered Quentin. Though it might be impossible—he'd tried for the last four weeks, with no success, to dissuade the determined unkindness from harassing him.

Brigham "Brig" Knight shook his head.

"We will be out of here in no time," Quentin assured his best friend as they dug up the ground near the head of the newly-buried corpse. *Baltimore really is the perfect spot for resurrectionists*, he thought while digging. *When the ground is frozen solid as a tombstone in New England and the Midwest, here a couple of fellows wielding spades and ropes can pay their bills.*

His thoughts were interrupted by the scrape of their metal shovel blades against wood. The raven audience screeched at the sound but didn't leave their nearby roosts.

"There is your coffin," said Brig.

From the resigned tone of his voice, Quentin knew his friend had given up arguing and would be on board for the rest of the night's activities. "Let's open her up. See what we've got."

After prying off the lid with a shovel blade, they looped a rope under the body's armpits. The casket's occupant was a young woman of slight stature. A real gem of a find—she'd be easy to drag from the box and lug to their cart.

Rather than secret their cart outside the North Avenue entrance to the Baltimore Cemetery, Quentin had bribed the guard to look the other way when they pushed-pulled it into the graveyard. Using the same designated paths as the gravediggers who brought the deceased to their final resting place for burial was not only easier but more efficient. They had a rendezvous time scheduled, therefore it was necessary to swiftly complete their task.

"What are we doing robbing graves? We are better than this," said Brig as they carried the dead girl.

"After tonight, we only need to *resurrect* another night's worth of corpses to pay for the rest of the school year." Quentin reminded his friend. "Then, it is no digging until next August. Unless we want to..."

"No!" responded Brig. "One more night, then absolutely no digging until summer."

Quentin sighed. It would be nice to have a little bit of spare change to court Brig's sister, Lenore, in better style. Unfortunately, his friend seemed set on halting their illegal nighttime exhumations. He supposed the last jug of whiskey he had used to bribe the Baltimore Cemetery guard would keep them in good stead until summer when they needed to resurrect more bodies.

After loading the young woman in their cart, Brig and he pushed her down the lane until they found another fresh grave. The grim birds followed.

A few minutes of digging removed enough dirt to expose a portion of the coffin's lid. Still not wholly committed to tonight's *resurrecting*, Brig stepped back from the wooden box. Quentin sighed, then pried open the lid and looped a rope around the corpse's neck. He would have preferred to tie the rope under the body's arms, but the man inside was large and tightly squeezed into the casket.

"Grab hold of your end of the rope," he ordered his reluctant partner in crime.

"Fine," muttered Brig as he grasped the thick sisal, wrapped it around his hand, and helped Quentin pull the heavy cadaver from its box.

Alas, while Brig and he were dragging the body out of the coffin, the man's head popped off. The grizzly body-part flew through the air, hit a nearby tombstone with a soggy thunk, then rolled to a stop by a metal flower urn. Luckily, the head didn't split open—though the skin on the neck was torn and there were cuts on the forehead where it had slammed into the headstone.

"Drat!" he exclaimed. "We won't get as much for him in two pieces.

A horrified Brig didn't answer him. He was staring at the head resting a few yards away with the back of his wrist pressed against his mouth as if he was stifling a scream. Whereas the unkindness of ravens who had been following them must have thought the unattached head a morbid joke, for they cackled loudly. Though he dared not say so out loud, Quentin suspected if they left the head alone for a minute or two with the villainous birds, they would come back to a skull picked clean of its flesh—outside and in.

"Come on," he urged. "We'll carry him to the cart with his head balanced on his chest. Then, you can watch the bodies while I go back and get the shovels.

Brig nodded as he grabbed the man's ankles. His best friend didn't utter a word while they carried the decapitated corpse. After placing the man and his head in the cart beside the girl, Quentin hurried back to the burial site to retrieve their tools. Then, followed by the unkindness, he returned to the cart.

Though silent, the ravens flapped above their heads as Brig and he wheeled the bodies to a nearby warehouse to meet Danny O'Connor. The unkindness cast an ominous shadow on the moonlit cobblestones at their feet.

"Those wicked birds know what we did," said Brig as they waited for Danny-O to slide open the warehouse's door.

"Listen to yourself—afraid of a few blackbirds. The ravens can't hurt us." Quentin wasn't the superstitious type but had to admit the staring unkindness was unsettling. He hoped his lighthearted words would shake off the feeling of doom which draped over this night's grave robbing like dark bunting. Before he could think of something else to say to cheer his friend up, the door slid open and a freckled-faced man of sixty-some years waved them inside the building.

"Got the barrels ready for you," said Danny. "You needing two or three?"

"Just two," responded Quentin. "I think this makes a dozen cadavers to load onto a boxcar and send off to New York."

"Baker's dozen would have made a better profit, but twelve will do," said Danny as he helped them wheel the bodies to a corner of the warehouse where three open barrels were partially filled with whiskey.

"Let's put the girl in first. She's smaller," suggested Quentin.

Danny surveyed the girls' body. He removed a ring, earrings, and locket, and slipped them into his trouser pocket. "I appreciate you boys letting me have the valuables."

"Just an extra reward for your help," replied Quentin. Keeping his thoughts to himself, he added in his mind, *We may be body-snatchers, but at least Brig and I don't steal from the dead.*

Brig said nothing, instead, he appeared to study his dirty fingernails.

It occurred to Quentin that his friend really was done with the *resurrecting* business. *What a shame*, he thought. *We've already earned a good deal of money, and there's more to be made.*

"Let's get her into the barrel," Quentin told Brig as he reached into the cart and slipped his hands under the girl's armpits.

Averting his eyes so he didn't have to look at the corpse's face, Brig helped him lift the girl, then fold her in half before placing her in the wooden barrel. Once she was inside, Danny filled the rest of the container with whiskey. Lastly, Danny placed the lid on top and hammered it in place.

"I'm betting they will be lined up for a jar of rot-gut whiskey from that barrel. Her being so fresh and all." Danny took off his cap, wiped his hair back, then replaced the cap. "This fellow won't be so easy to stuff in a barrel," he said jerking his thumb toward the decapitated corpse. "'Course the head being separate makes it a little easier."

"That is what I was thinking." Quentin was a practical person. No matter how unfeeling the statement sounded, the corpulent man was already dead. It didn't really matter if his head was attached.

Danny did his usual valuables search. He pocketed a watch and ring, then observed, "He's going to be a lot to wrangle. Even with whiskey lubricating things, it is going to be a tight squeeze. We'll be lucky if the three of us can do it without help."

His evaluation of the situation proved correct. Getting the dead man off the cart, folded up, and squished into the barrel required the strength of all three men. Once the body was in the wooden container, Quentin pushed the head into the largest unoccupied area.

"Didn't need as much whiskey to fill this barrel," said Danny as he hammered the lid on the second container. "But folks will still line up for a stiff drink from this one, too."

"And the alcohol will keep everybody in good shape until they reach the New York medical schools," said Quentin as he brushed some graveyard dirt from his pants.

"And keep the stink of decay down," added Danny with a laugh.

Quentin glanced at Brig's face. His friend looked like he wanted to cry. No more chatting with the whiskey dealer. It was time to head home. "Gentlemen, we've done our good deed for the night. Medical schools will have bodies to train doctors, and no one living was harmed. Let's go, Brig, time for some shut-eye."

"Boys, I'm sending these barrels out on a train in two days time. If you want to bring me a couple more stiffs tomorrow, I've still got room," said Danny. "If you don't show up, Old Danny-O will figure these twelve are all..."

Whatever the whiskey dealer meant to say next was drowned out by the squawks and screeches of the unkindness of ravens. Somehow, they had managed to enter the warehouse. The unfriendly birds were circling above the trio of body-smugglers making enough racket that someone was sure to come investigate.

"We are out of here," Quentin called over his shoulder as he and Brig fled out the door, down the cobblestone streets, and finally into the entrance of the building where he rented a small apartment. He noticed the unkindness abandoned the warehouse, choosing instead to follow Brig and him. As they entered his building, he saw the dismal birds settle on the rooftop of the storefront across the street.

***

"We're going to get caught," Brig said the next afternoon as they sat in Quentin's apartment. "Both of us need to finish our studies at the university and get real jobs. I don't want to get tossed out of college for robbing graves."

"We are not likely to get caught," responded Quentin as he looked between the purple curtains hanging in the front room's windows at a lone raven perched outside on top of a stone gargoyle. "Even if we do, they rarely prosecute. If they do decide to make an example of us, it is only a misdemeanor. The University will probably ignore the whole business."

"I hope you're right," said Brig in a voice that still carried a hint of worry. He ran his forefinger across the top of a small marble bust of Athena which Quentin kept on a table by the window. "What if Lenore finds out?"

That was a bigger problem for Quentin. He was in love with Brig's younger sister, Lenore. After he graduated with a medical degree, he intended to make her his wife.

He suspected she would never understand that the shortage of funds to pay for his education made his *resurrectionist* activities necessary. And necessary for her brother as well.

"If it will make you feel better, we'll only *resurrect* two bodies tonight. We haven't dug at Greenmount Cemetery in a while, so no one will be looking for us there. I've got a bottle of rot-gut to give to the caretaker, so we should be in and out quick as a wink." Quentin winked at his best friend for emphasis.

"Sounds good to me," said Brig before patting Athena's marble helmet. "But I still have a bad feeling about this whole business."

"Don't worry. Everything is under control," Quentin assured Brig before looking out the window at the raven who had shifted position, and now, peered through the wavy glass at Brig, the statue of Athena, and him.

***

That night started like dozens before—Brig and he entering a cemetery searching for freshly-covered graves. Unfortunately, an unkindness of ravens waited for them at the front gate of Greenmount Cemetery. As they walked about the graveyard, the ebony birds seemed determined to flutter above and beside them clicking their beaks. Quentin wondered if it was the same group of ravens from the previous night—the same unkindness who had been shadowing him for weeks. Not that it mattered. A flock of birds was nothing more than a flock of birds after all.

Nevertheless, he didn't say anything about his suspicions, lest he spook his already nervous friend.

Pushing their cart loaded with two shovels, they wheeled their way down a path towards the center of Greenmount Cemetery where the caretaker told them several people had been buried in the last few days.

Rot-gut always does the job, thought Quentin. Of course, the cemetery's guard didn't know the alcohol had been used to preserve a body. And he felt no compunction to inform the caretaker of the source of the whiskey. Besides, a bribe recipient can't complain about the quality of his bribe to the authorities. He would be testifying against himself!

When they arrived at the area mentioned by the cemetery's guard, in addition to a mound of raw earth, they spotted an above-ground mausoleum with its door ajar. As luck would have it, there was a fresh wreath on the gate, a scattering of flower petals outside the door, and footprints still visible in the soft earth beside the brick walkway. It was clear that someone had been newly-interred.

"Look here," said Brig as he swung open the cast-iron gate surrounding the crypt and walked to its entrance. "This will be a quick *resurrection*. Though tonight can't go by quick enough for me."

The words were no sooner out of his mouth, then a deathly pale hand reached from the depths of the building, grabbed Brig's shoulder, and yanked him into the mausoleum.

"Quentin," he screamed as he was dragged into the tomb. "Help me."

Quentin froze. He wanted to rescue his best friend, but he was afraid of whatever had attacked Brig. The agitated croaks and caws of the unkindness of ravens perched around him on the wrought iron fence brought him back to his senses. He ran to the mausoleum's door, lifted his lantern, and scanned the interior. A man dressed in dark clothing crouched over Brig.

"Hey!" shouted Quentin. "What do you think..."

"Leave," hissed the man as he looked up.

The gore dripping from his mouth and the two bone-white canines glinting in the lantern's light silenced any protest Quentin might have made. His eyes fell on Brig's neck. Not only had the undead creature bitten it—he had ripped his friend's neck open. Based on his anatomy classes, it was clear to him from the amount of blood spilling from the gash that there was no saving Brig. Still, he couldn't leave without trying to do something.

Quentin ran, grabbed one of the shovels from their cart, returned to the crypt, and rushed toward the vampire.

With a noise that sounded like the blend of a laugh and croak, the vampire released Brig's body. Then, he twirled and exploded into a flock of ravens which joined the unkindness still waiting on the fencing. Together, the mass of inky birds flew skyward leaving Quentin to figure out what to do next.

I can't be caught here with a body in that condition, thought Quentin. *I will surely be charged with murder.* That is when a plan began to form in his mind. He would load Brig into the cart, wheel him down to the dock area, empty his pockets, dump him in an alleyway, then wheel the cart containing nothing but two shovels back to Danny-O's warehouse. If he met the whiskey dealer, he'd tell him Brig never showed, so there will be no more cadavers until next summer. Then, tomorrow, or maybe even tonight, dockworkers or boatmen would find Brig. Everyone would assume his friend was the victim of an especially violent robbery.

"This could work," he told Brig as he loaded his friend's body into the cart between the shovels. He paused a moment, looked at Brig's face, closed his best friend's eyes with his fingers, and sighed.

"I'm sorry," he whispered before wheeling the still-warm body toward the docks.

***

Though devastated by Brigham's murder, the Knight family set to the task of preparing his damaged body for a viewing in their parlor. Out of respect for Brig's parents, and because he loved his friend and his friend's sister, Quentin assisted with the body prep.

"A body should be prepared by loving hands," said Mrs. Knight as she gently washed her son. "But I didn't know what to do about the neck injury." She paused to wipe her eyes and nose on a handkerchief. "Thank you for agreeing to…"

"I am happy I was able to help," said Quentin as he finished stitching Brig's neck wound closed. Glad he had the surgical skill to patch his friend up, he was amazed at the amount of damaged the vampire had done. Of course, the savage biting and tearing employed by the undead creature to access the jugular meant there wasn't the legendary, two-fang, bite mark visible.

Quentin was the only person who knew a vampire was the real killer. Which meant he was a liability to the murderous creature. Therefore, when Mrs. Knight insisted he eat dinner with the family and spend the night so he could stand by Lenore at tomorrow's viewing, Quentin agreed. He felt safer with others around. It would take a bold vampire to enter a home filled with people.

After Brig's body was dressed in his finest jacket and trousers with a black scarf strategically wrapped around his neck, Mrs. Knight walked Quentin to the door to Brig's third-floor bedroom. "He always thought so much of you, dear. I think he would be comforted to know you slept in his room," she explained.

"Thank you," he responded, though he felt the hairs on the back of his neck stand up when he entered the candle-lit room.

The reason for the sudden chill racing up and down his spine was immediately evident. Someone had left the window open. The early December air was too cold for such a mistake. But as Quentin strode across the room to close the window, he saw a black feather fall to the floor at his feet. Whirling around, he came face to face with the vampire from Greenmount Cemetery.

"We meet again," said the undead creature.

Quentin took a step back. "How did you get in? We are on the third..."

The vampire smiled. "As if you don't know."

The ravens, thought Quentin. *He travels as an unkindness of ravens.* Suddenly, another thought came to him, *the vampire might be immune to sunlight if he is in raven-form. Which means I will never be safe from him.*

"I see you're beginning to realize how much danger you're in," said the vampire. "But I am a reasonable man, as I hope you are."

"You are no longer a man," said Quentin.

"I suppose you're right." The undead creature waved one of his whiter-than-a-winding-sheet hands. "But I was a mortal man once. Currently, I am known in Baltimore as Garridan Ardelean. A role I like. If someone should threaten that position, I would be forced to..."

"Your secret is safe with me," Quentin promised the vampire, though it galled him to speak with the creature who'd murdered Brig

"I'm not here tonight to speak of secrets," said Ardelean. "It's a time of mourning for you. I'm not so far removed from my humanity that I don't know that. So, mourn your friend. But tomorrow, we must talk."

Wondering why the vampire hadn't killed him already, Quentin nodded. "Thank you for your..." He paused. Quentin didn't know what word to finish the statement with. Kindness? Patience? Understanding? None of those terms seemed right for someone who'd killed Quentin's best friend.

"Save your thank-yous until you have heard my offer. Because your word is not enough. I will need more than promises to safeguard my position in the city as a prosperous merchant of Romanian birth who deals in gems and antiquities," replied Garridan Ardelean. With that, he moved to the window, open it, then transformed into a flock of ravens. Thereupon, the darker-than-a-tomb unkindness circled around Quentin for a few seconds before swooping out the window.

Weak in the knees, Quentin managed to close the window before collapsing on the bed. Still fully clothed, he wrapped the blankets and quilt around himself and willed his body to stop shaking as he gazed at the glowing embers in the bedroom's fireplace. He was afraid to learn what more the prosperous merchant of Romanian birth needed from him.

***

Brig's burial day was a blur. His mind swirled with images of visitors paying respects to Brigham Knight and his family, the funeral, the walk to the cemetery, the internment, and the meal afterward. Finally, all had departed the Knight's home save for the family, their servants, and Quentin. He knew Mrs. Knight would invite him to spend another night in Brig's room if he lingered much longer, but he needed to return to his apartment and think.

"I must be getting home," Quentin said as he embraced Mr. and Mrs. Knight.

"You could stay," offered Brig's mother.

"No, thank you," he replied. "I think it's best if I go home and get back to my studies."

Brig's parents nodded, then left the room—leaving Lenore and him to say their farewells.

"Lenore, these last few days have made me realize how much I care for..."

"No," said Brig's golden-haired sister. "Do not ask me questions or put any sort of pressure upon me." She raised her doe-eyes to look him square in the face. "After a period of mourning, I shall again think about the future. But for now, I am too deep in sorrow and focused on memories to consider anything else."

The beautiful Lenore stood, took a step toward Quentin, then laid one fine-boned hand on his arm. "Dear Quentin, I love you as a brother. I cannot promise that I will feel otherwise in time. You need to move forward without me."

Though her words were like a stake to his heart, still he held a smile on his lips and murmured, "I shall always love you, Lenore. As I shall always love your brother and your family."

With a tear trickling down her perfect, ivory cheek, she stood on tiptoe and kissed him first on one side of his mouth, then on the other. But she never placed her lips upon his.

"Goodbye," he said in a voice full of woe. Then, he stepped back, bowed slightly, donned his hat, and left the Knight home.

No sooner had he set foot on the cobblestones then a black-garbed Garridan Ardelean joined him on his stroll.

"There are things we need to discuss," said the Romanian merchant.

Quentin noted that Garridan wore gloves, a cape with an upturned collar, and a wide-brimmed hat. Thus, even though the late-afternoon sun was still out, none of its dimming light struck the vampire's skin.

"Can't it wait?"

"I'm afraid not," responded Garridan. "Here is my proposal: either you join my family, or we take Lenore. Either way, you will be certain to guard our secret."

"Our?" *How many vampires were wandering the streets of Baltimore*, he wondered.

"My wife and I. The rest of the family remained in Europe."

"You cannot have Lenore," Quentin stated. "She deserves a life filled with joy after what has happened. I won't allow it."

The vampire laughed. "You have no power to stop us. But I've decided to give you a choice." The Romanian merchant's voice took on a more serious tone as he continued, "My wife, Miriana, and I plan to establish a family in America. She spied you on one of your graveyard expeditions and has been following you ever since. She'd already decided that you must come to live with us, when I, in a weak moment, took the life of your friend."

"The ravens!" he gasped. It all made sense now. He hadn't considered the unkindness had been following him since early November. He *was* being stalked. He halted in front of his apartment building. "Can you enter if I don't invite you in?"

"That is nothing but folklore," said Garridan with a grin as he stepped into the building. "As is the business of crosses and holy water."

***

For two days, Quentin sat in his apartment in his favorite chair, an unread book on his lap. Garridan sat opposite him, near the statue of Athena, staring at the flames flickering in the apartment's small fireplace. Suddenly, a lone raven flew in through the partially opened window and perched on the elaborate frieze above the door.

Its vines, fruits, flowers, and woodland animals formed of wood and plaster jutted out far enough to give the obsidian corvid a comfortable and intimidating roost. Using its coal-black beak, the bird leaned down and tapped on the door frame.

"Welcome, my love," said the Romanian merchant to the raven.

The bird turned her shining eyes to look at him. "Garridan," she said before resuming her tapping.

"Why are you tapping at the door?" asked Quentin.

The raven who was Garridan's wife opened her beak and spoke. "I am reminding you of time passing. As it passes, I am reminding you of death approaching. Mortals must heed the tick of the clock, but not the Family Corb-a-Codru."

"Family Corb-a-Codru? I thought you said your name was Ardelean." Quentin shifted his gaze to Garridan.

"Ardelean serves us well at the moment," explained Garridan as he ran his fingers around his hat's brim, "but our family's true name is Corb-a-Codru—Raven of the Forest."

The raven who was Garridan's wife resumed her tapping.

"The minutes are ticking. It is time for you to accept Miriana and I as your parents. It should not be difficult, as your human parents are both deceased."

A niggling in the back of Quentin's brain whispered, *the Ravens of the Forest might have had something to do with the carriage accident that sent Mother and Father over a cliff all those years ago. An unkindness could certainly have spooked the horses. The driver was killed, also, so there are no living witnesses to the event.*

Though the room was warm, he shivered. He wondered if the Romanian couple were capable of such long-term planning. Would they be willing to implement a well-orchestrated action years earlier to get what they wanted now? His heart wanted the answer to be: *no.* But his mind knew it could be: *yes.*

"I'm happy being a mortal," said Quentin. *Be careful of what you say,* he reminded himself before continuing. "And though she doesn't yet love me, I hope to marry Lenore Knight. If I join the Family Corb-a-Codru, I cannot..."

"Lenore is lost to you," stated the vampire. "You may mourn her for all your days if you wish, but it will not bring her back into your life unless you want her to join our family, too."

"No. Leave her out of our bargain," said Quentin. He would rather lose Lenore than for countless years witness her draining the blood of innocents. His fate would never be hers. He sighed. "Lenore is now no more than a youthful dream to me. I alone will join your family."

"Splendid!" said Garridan as he stood and nodded to the raven atop the door frame. "My dear..."

The raven leapt from her perch. As Quentin watched, the one bird seemed to split, then split again and again until twenty ravens swirled in front of him in a blur of sinister feathers. Then, with a noise like wind whistling down a chimney, the birds coalesced into a slender woman garbed in an obsidian, silk gown.

"Quentin," said the woman looking at him with eyes the color of honey as she extended her hand, "I am Miriana Ardelean of the Family Corb-a-Codru."

"Madam." He stood, then gingerly shook her hand. "It appears you know me well, though I am just now making your acquaintance."

She smiled—her whiter-than-starlight teeth showing between lips as red as heart's blood. "It is always best to get to know someone before making him your son. I find a decade or more is necessary," she replied. Then, still holding his eyes with hers, she stepped closer, leaned in, and bit his neck.

He was shocked! After a split second of pain, no more than a bee sting, Quentin felt a warmth surge through his veins. It was like the first sip of hot tea going down the throat or the comfort of a quilt wrapped around you as you sat by the fire. And then, it was fire. Fire heating his whole body. He felt more alive—as if he had been living a half-life up to this moment.

He suddenly realized Miriana had moved to stand by Garridan. The vampire couple studied him as he looked at the world through new eyes.

"What has happened?"

"You are changed," explained Garridan.

"I took a sip of your blood and replaced it with mine," said Miriana. "The Family Corb-a-Codru is strong. Strong enough to flow through your veins and transform all of your blood to ours. Now, you truly are our son."

Based on his medical training, her words seemed impossible, but based on the burning sensation throughout his arteries and veins, Quentin knew she spoke the truth. He glanced about the apartment where he and Brig had spent so many happy hours. It wasn't home any longer. His forever home was wherever Miriana and Garridan were.

"What next, Mother? Father?" he asked.

"Spin and think of wings," said his new mother as she twirled into a flock of ravens.

Garridan opened the window before he followed suit.

Outside in the dreary air, a cloud of ravens fluttered—waiting.

Quentin stared at the fireplace one final time, thinking of Brig and Lenore. But rather than lend a cheerfulness to the midnight hour, the crackling fire sent fantastical shadows crawling across the floor toward his feet.

"The past is gone," he at last admitted. Though he suspected he'd haunt Baltimore Cemetery, Greenmount

Cemetery, and the docks, warehouses, alleyways, and churchyards of Baltimore for decades. "Decades!" he whispered. "More like centuries."

Saying those words, no matter how macabre, made the next step easier. He thought of soaring on ebon wings, stretched out his arms, and began to twirl like a whirlwind. A feeling of limitless energy washed over him. He locked eyes with one of the ravens on the other side of the window. Then, as Quentin felt the vampire blood pounding beneath his skin, he burst into an unkindness and followed his parents into the Baltimore night—forevermore.

Author Bio

Vonnie Winslow Crist, HWA, SFWA, is author of *The Enchanted Dagger, Owl Light, The Greener Forest, Murder on Marawa Prime,* and other award-winning books. Her stories appear in *Chilling Ghost Short Stories, Cast of Wonders, Amazing Stories, SLAY: Stories of the Vampire Noire, Killing It Softly 2, Blood & Beetles, Horror for Hire: First Shift, Creep, Mother Ghost's Grimm 1 & 2, Devolution Z, Monsters, Scary Snippets: Halloween, Re-Terrify, Samhain Secrets, Forest of Fear, Re-Haunt, Coffins & Dragons,* and elsewhere. Still believing the world is filled with mystery, miracles, and magic, Vonnie strives to celebrate the power of myth in her writing.

Black Cats & Ravens

By Eddie D. Moore

I haven't always lived at the orphanage. In fact, I used to have a normal life and family just like most other people. My story isn't long, but most people tend to think that I'm making it up. I can tell by the look in their eyes that they often stop listening to me before I'm even halfway through, but I'll tell it again if you'll promise to hear me out.

It was a chilly November morning two weeks after my thirteenth birthday, and I was snuggled deep inside my blankets when I heard a slow tap, tap, tap at the window next to my bed. Ignoring the annoyance at my window, I tried to bury my head deeper into my pillow. The rooster crowed, and I knew it wouldn't be long before my mother came to chase me out of my warm sanctuary to face my daily chores.

I felt myself dozing off again when a loud squawk startled me and sent shivers down my spine. With a sigh, I rolled over to look out the window that was just a few inches from my face. I blinked as a large raven pecked the glass pane. The bird's sinister eyes were filled with malice as it tapped harder upon the glass, and I reflexively backed away.

The wood floor was cold upon my bare feet, and the brisk morning air filled my skin with goosebumps. Long seconds passed as the beast and I stared into each other's eyes. I felt like the bird was looking directly into my soul and I had to look away. I dropped my gaze as the raven pecked at something near its feet. I gaped at what I saw. A large eye that looked eerily human was lying at the bird's feet and my heart pounded faster at the sight of it. A long stringy piece of flesh hung behind it, and I felt my stomach twist in knots inside me as it stared at me with its dead pupil. The raven stepped upon the grotesque sight before me and pecked at it between taps and squawks at my window.

I don't have the vocabulary to describe the terror that grew inside me each time the bird stopped to look at me. Even though I considered myself a grown man, the shout for my mother felt very natural as I left my room. The tone of my cries must've carried my fear and desperation for both my mother and father immediately came running up the stairs and asking what was wrong.

Words failed me, and I couldn't at that moment find my voice to answer, so I pointed through my doorway. My father charged passed me as my mother wrapped her comforting arms around me and whispered soothing assurances into my ear. I pressed my face against her shirt collar and swallowed the giant lump stuck in my throat. I waited several long moments to hear my father's exclamations of astonishment or wonder, but they never came.

When I turned my head, my father was leaning against the door frame, shaking his head. I glanced out my window, but the bird and the horrid eye were gone.

Leafless trees and clouds heavy with potential rain were the only sights to see on that dismal morning. Grumbling to himself, my father descended the stairs and returned to his breakfast. My mother, God rest her soul, rested a reassuring hand on my shoulder a moment before following my father.

Later that morning, my mother received a telegram that was delivered by the local sheriff. I'll never forget the expression on her face as she read the message. She let the telegram drop to the floor and walked out of the house without saying a word. I saw a teardrop roll off her cheek before the door closed behind her. My father picked up the message and grunted before sticking it into his pocket and mumbling something to himself.

Knowing she was upset, I thought my father would go try to console my mother, but instead, he sat down at the kitchen table and drummed his fingers on the tabletop impatiently. The closer it came to lunchtime, the madder he got. I worked up the nerve once to ask him what was wrong. The curses and threats that followed were enough to persuade me to stay out of sight until my mother returned. It was nearly dinner time when she finally walked through the front door. The violent argument that ensued between them answered all of my questions.

The telegram was sent to notify my mother that her sister's body had been found walled up in the basement of her home. Her husband, my father's brother, had been convicted of her murder and was scheduled to be executed that evening. When I peeked into the kitchen, it broke my heart to see my mother sobbing and shaking uncontrollably. My aunt and uncle were both animal lovers. It was hard for me to imagine that my uncle was capable of murder, but judging by my parent's argument, my mother had no such reservations.

When my father stomped out the back door, my mother started cleaning as she always did when she was upset. I carefully walked back up the stairs so that my mother wouldn't know that I'd been eavesdropping. From my bedroom window, I watched my father as he worked through his anger with a long-handled scythe. He slashed ruthlessly at a patch of brush that he had been planning on clearing for several seasons. He'd stop every few minutes and take a drink from a bottle of whiskey that he usually kept hidden from my mother.

I noticed a black cat in the woods watching my father. When it turned its head the right direction, I could see a small white patch on its chest. My father hated cats, and in his current mood, I knew that he wouldn't hesitate to kill the cat if he saw it. Fearing that I wouldn't reach the cat in time, I ran downstairs and ignored my mother's shouts as I let the back door slam closed behind me.

My father grumbled something as I passed him, but I was determined to frighten away the cat before my father noticed it and did something horrible. Just before the creature turned to run from my approach, I saw that it was missing an eye. I stopped at the edge of the tree line and wondered for a moment if it was the cat's eye that the raven had brought to my window that morning, but the pupil on the eye I saw through my window was round. I heard footsteps and turned to see who it was just as my father backhanded me across my left cheek.

The next thing I remember was the taste of blood and spitting out dirt and small pieces of dried leaves. My father shouted at me about playing games instead of growing up. He raised the scythe above his head, and I instinctively shut my eyes and threw up my arms in a feeble attempt to protect myself. A few moments passed and nothing happened. I heard the squawk of a raven and cracked open my eyes just in time to see the large bird pluck my father's eye from its socket.

The bird flew high into the treetops. Between my father's screams, I could hear the bird gloating over its newly won prize with an eerie cackle that sounded like laughter. My mother ran across the yard while my father held a bloody hand over his face and screamed at the ground. I'll never forget the concern in my mother's eyes when she stopped and rested a gentle hand on my father's shoulder. An instant later, my father buried the scythe in my mother's skull.

I'll never be able to scrub the gory image from my mind. At least four inches of the scythe came out the other side of her head, and I couldn't tear my eyes away from its blood-soaked edge. The next thing I knew, my father was on top of me, and his hands wrapped around my throat. I couldn't breathe and time seemed to slow.

I saw the one-eyed cat staring at us from a tree limb above. It seemed satisfied and relaxed. I'm not sure if I was imagining it or not, but I believe, the beast was purring as it watched. The edges of my vision began to darken, and I remember my father mumbling about not being hanged if there weren't any witnesses.

With considerable effort, I managed to get an arm free and drove my thumb into my father's empty eye socket. I gasped for air as I wrestled myself free. Once I was on my feet, I ran into the woods. The trees and underbrush became a blur as I ran. My father stumbled behind me shouting and cursing as I put more distance between us.

I was running down a deer trail when the black cat suddenly dashed across my path causing me to stumble and trip. I felt something in my right ankle tear as I fell to the ground. My father shouted my name over and over in the distance as the raven squawked and jumped around in the tree limbs above me. It felt as though the bird was trying to lead my father to me, and as his shouts came closer, I knew that I'd have to try running again.

Painfully, I stood up and tried putting one foot in front of the other. I held my breath each time I put weight on my right foot. Every other step was pure agony. After about twenty steps, I fell back to the ground panting. The raven continued to excitedly dance from limb to limb as night fell around me. I found a fat tree limb to use as a crutch and slowly hobbled my way deeper into the forest.

My nose and fingers grew numb as the temperature dropped around me. I'm not sure if hours passed or minutes, but eventually, I just couldn't go any further. When I found a fallen tree blocking my path, I took shelter from the wind by lying down and crawling underneath it. The ground was cold, but the tree blocked most of the wind and gave me plenty of cover from unwelcome eyes.

I heard footsteps rustling the dead leaves deep in the night, and I held my breath knowing that if my father found me that I had no escape. From my hiding place, I saw the one-eyed cat stop a few feet from me. Its eye reflected the moonlight, and it slow blinked at me as if to softly say, I found you. We stared at each other as my father shouted my name with a dry voice and came closer to my hiding spot.

The cat hissed and growled, and my father's footsteps fell silent. I hadn't seen or heard the raven for hours, but I could hear it now high in the treetops. The rustle of leaves started again and came closer. I felt a warm tear roll down my cheek, and I tried to make myself smaller. I considered dashing out from under the tree, but I knew that there was no way that I could outrun my father on my ankle.

Once my father was standing in front of my hiding place, the cat began to purr loudly, and the raven fell silent. I had completely forgotten that my father hated cats, and with a hate-filled curse, he swung the scythe at the cat. The cat wasted no time trying to distance itself from my father, and he chased after it in a blind rage.

I let out a relieved sigh as I heard my father's shouts fade in the distance. A silence so complete fell around me that I began to wonder if I had suddenly become deaf. Slowly, the sounds of the night returned. The scrape of bare tree limbs rubbing together in the wind sung me a lullaby, and I drifted off to sleep as a lone owl hooted nearby.

I awoke to the sound of a woodpecker searching for his morning breakfast. I quietly scooted out from under the fallen tree. The wisps of fog still hung in the air. My biggest fear was discovering that my father had returned while I slept and was waiting nearby. I relaxed when I saw that the cat, raven, and my father were nowhere to be seen.

It took hours for me to find my way out of the forest, but eventually, I recognized where I was and limped to the Clemm's farm. They sent for the local sheriff. The search for my father continued for days. The dogs lost his trail deep in the woods by the fallen tree I sheltered under. He was never seen again.

My mother's funeral was three days later, and a few short hours after that, I was given a bed here at the orphanage. No one believes my story when I tell them the part the cat and raven played in my tale. They just give me that look of indulgence and nod as if they somehow understand what I went through. No one here understands what I experienced that night, and I doubt anyone ever will.

My fear of ravens and black cats is considered superstitious by the nuns running the orphanage. When I refuse to go outside, Sr. Mary Vianney often locks me in the spandrel and tells me to pray. Once she discovered that being locked in a dark closed place made me feel safe, she started using her cane on my back to drive me outside.

I don't know what I'll do when I have to leave the orphanage, but for the time being, they can beat and punish me all they want as long as I can stay away from black cats and ravens. They might not all be evil, but why risk it?

Keep your distance from both of them. Heed my tale and take my advice—forevermore.

Author Bio:

Eddie D. Moore travels hundreds of hours a year, and he fills that time by listening to audiobooks. When he isn't playing with his grandchildren, he writes his own twisted tales. He has published two mini-anthologies: After Storming Area 51 and Misfits & Oddities. You can find his stories in dozens of other anthologies and scattered around the web.

RHAPSODIE De CLAIRE ELISE

by Sue Marie St. Lee

My conception, a result of copulation between my father and mother, was nothing more than a consequence of their lust for one another and I became consequence number four. There would be more consequences after me, five more to be exact. There is no doubt that even more consequences would have come into this world except for the fact that while birthing consequence-number-nine, Mother died.

Her death brought no direct effect on my life. I continued my schooling and when old enough, entered the New England Conservatory to further my prodigious talent as a violinist and composer. I looked forward to learning how to put down on paper my compositions, which from the time I was five years old, opus played and stored continually in my brain.

Even now, as I tell you this, a butterfly's wings fluttering outside my window on the lilac bush are composing a sonata in my brain. It is a beautiful movement of complementary chords and scattered singular notes, airy and light, a bit breezy and free until I hear the praying mantis approach. Darkness finds its way into my arrangement as the butterfly struggles for its life. Bass chords pound out of tune while treble notes tinkle with great ferocity until they slow to a dying cadence. There,

there it is, the final chord of this, the first movement of my sonata, Beauté Dévorée.

That is how it happens, how I create incomparable sonatas. Life only makes sense to me through music, it is the universal language of mathematical schemes. My compositions are stories without words, I declare my magnum opus — Rhapsodie de Claire Elise — Claire Elise, whom I met while performing with the Philadelphia Orchestra. Claire Elise, my beautiful, wondrous, melodious sylph — the first woman to play with an orchestra in the United States.

The moment my eyes set gaze upon her, music such that only has been heard in Heaven filled my head and it came from her. Never had I seen such an aura of music surround anyone or anything — it emanated from within her. She was music incarnate. With her in my life, I would write my greatest adagio. Mankind would behold the melodies of Claire Elise for all time and beyond the heavens and stars.

Her soul's melody drove me to write my infamous Violin Concerto in D major opus 27. Many times have I played the creation as only the composer can; yet, when I asked Conductor Stokowski to give the solo piece to Claire, I never imagined her interpretation to exceed my composition's glory to the height whereto it ascended. She took center stage, playing with such passion, I saw tears weep from the violin's bout while droplets of blood floated from the strings to the floor. I saw more of the music than I had created — than I ever could have imagined. How is it that she could improve on the musical ecstasy to which I alone gave life? I would come to know the answer as I studied her ambiance over the next year.

No matter the piece Claire played, solo or accompanied, her magnificent execution materialized the music — into color before my eyes. Colors of every hue, depth, brilliance — more colors than have been realized in imagination or sight. They became fluid in their efforts, colored waves rushing from rocky streams in sunlight, moonlight, even through my darkest chords, they glistened through my blackness.

She took great delight when performing a descant, as I took great delight in writing them above the melody's theme for her to fulfill as only she could. I watched the vibrations in her aura change color and intensity with each stroke of the bow and position of her fingers as they staccatoed across the strings. I studied her substance with the ferocity of a crazed, hungry predator, wanting to know the exactness of the source from which her beauteous witchcraft was borne as it could only be witchcraft that drove her to translate that of my perfection to an even greater pinnacle.

Month after month, performance after performance, no matter the pieces created by the greats such as Rachmaninoff, Beethoven, Tchaikovsky, or the incomparable Mozart, she exuded mastery. No auditorium, location or season, could confound her brilliance. Claire… mysterious, beast of rendering, I must know, I must have that final piece of perfection as my own.

I noted, it is not the manner in which she insists upon the strings from her bow to produce such exaltation. I have studied this and know it not to be true. Might it be her strings? I know it not to be her instrument, for mine is Stradivarius, the champion of man-made structures that charm the absolute *ne plus ultra* from any instrument between the heavens and earth.

If not strings nor instrument, I must be certain. I must deduce whether, in fact, it be witchcraft or another power conveyed from a universal knowledge or realm. I set my plan into place for it should be easier to eliminate my witchcraft theory than anything from the universe. And, to my good fortune from my family's history of suspected ancestral witches, I knew the infinite test whereby to identify one's eternally damned soul as a witch.

My small, rural estate bordered a local meat production facility. Yes, my property, though presenting a quaint Victorian facade, did, on occasion smell of the foul remnants of blood and guts when the wind might discern to blow toward my humble abode. Perhaps that is why I was able to purchase it at such a low cost. Never the mind, it suited my purpose, and scarcely did I spend time outdoors to flavor the winds.

There would be cats, mongrels, opossums, raccoons, and other such vermin feasting on the smorgasbord of intestines and minuscule pieces of meat struggling to adhere together in the rancid stream dripping from the meat facility. I knew that I should find a black cat within this banquet. And, there, amidst the growling dogs who admonished my approach, I found him. Black as the night in a liquid nightmare, his fur did glisten in the starlight only to be outdone by his glowing green eyes.

I held out a freshly killed rat which I procured from my secondary root cellar by way of using a tire iron. The fresh blood caught his attention, as did the others in the gathering to whom I focused a threatening torch. Hortico, I chose his name before I ever met him, ran to the bait in my outheld hand. Leery, he circled the treasure until I stripped some meat from the cadaver and dropped it in front of him. That is how Hortico and I bonded as he followed me back to my home, dropping bits of flesh along the way. We secured our relationship over the next three months. Hortico's loyalty could not be surpassed.

Two items remained for which I must guarantee before I could certainly test the witch — chicken feathers and holy water. I would return to the meat plant and gather stray fowl feathers throughout the following months until acquiring enough to fashion a boa. After bleaching them, I soaked them in waters from the streams of blood seeping into shallow pools from the meatpacking plant. When dried they presented the most pleasant shade of pink that women adore. I strung them together to offer as a gift when Claire would come to visit at my home before playing Beethoven's Sonata No.9; Op. 47 in A Major.

One last detail… at Sunday Mass, I brought a small glass vial in which to collect holy water. Upon my return home, I called to Hortico, who trusted my every command. Holding him dearly to my chest, I held the glass eye-dropper above his sparkling green eyes and dropped not more than one drop onto them each. He didn't resist and licked my thumb afterward.

During these few months of Claire's first year with the orchestra, specific to after my curiosity engaged upon her mysterious endowment, she visited my home on many occasions as I invited her to practice new pieces I had written. Upon her first visit, her eyes scrutinized my home's barren atmosphere — not barren of furniture, barren of foofaraw which, I believe, stems from embellishments adorning tabletops, walls, mantles, and the like from a need of companionship. I saw no sense in hanging tatted lace window coverings. For what? What purpose could they possibly behold to me other than block a clear vision to the outdoors, which from behind my windows, appear as unequaled art painted with God's hand? Without having to change paintings or pictures, my window frames present nature's moods day-to-day, moment-by-moment, whether it be sunshine upon the fountain in my front garden, or moonbeams flittering through willow branches outside my bedroom. This is not to say my windows have no coverings at all. No. To say so would be to lie. Above my windows hang very thick, heavy velvet draperies colored as a midnight blue. They serve a distinct purpose when drawn together — to block everything out or keep what is already in — in.

On the occasion of that first visit, after Claire accustomed herself to my unpretentious yet fully-functional decorating scheme, I escorted her through the empty hallway to the library where my liquor cabinet, endowed with brandies, wines, and liqueurs in their original bottles, stood proudly. Again, I have no use for such amenities as crystal decanters. They would neither sweeten the taste of their contents nor cause its nectar to pour any smoother. Claire chose Cointrea. A fine selection, I concurred with a glass for myself as well.

While sipping our drinks, I offered to show the rest of my home to satisfy Claire's unspoken, yet innate female curiosity, of how the other rooms may also be spared of decorative personality other than practicality. The tour, devoid of conversation conjured from distracting froufrou, we returned to the library where I offered another drink which Claire declined and I suggested we go to the cellar where we would practice my Concerto.

Leading her down the hall from where we walked moments before, I gestured to the door under the second-floor stairs, opened it, flicked on the light switch, and motioned for her to follow me down the narrow steps to the cellar. She marveled that not one of the steps creaked and wondered at the overwhelming, haunting silence which filled the room. Her exact words were, "… the silence is suffocating…", to which I explained how I had insulated the room for not only acoustic properties but to control humidity which is imperative for properly storing my Stradivarius — as well as fabricating the strings for it. Her eyes grew large with contemplation as she thought out loud of how unique it was for a violinist to painstakingly create their own catgut. I retorted that my strings are not sourced from typical four-legged animals — sheep, goat, cattle, mules, hogs, or horses. I confessed that over the many years of testing different animal intestines, I discovered the strength and tenacity of owl intestines to render the most consistent tones which seemed to season my performances with scents of the night.

Halloween arrived with frigid winds which fought to keep the passenger door of my '31 Buick Eight closed as I struggled to open and steady it for Claire's leave from the vehicle. To ward off the changing season's chill, she donned a white-fox hip-length jacket over an ankle-length satin gown in white. It was one of my favorites. I had asked her to wear this gown for our private rehearsal at my home. It was imperative, you see, that when administering the witch-test, the suspect is clothed in white. Her white satin high-heeled shoes clicked out a rhythm as we made our way up the front porch steps through the entryway to the foyer where she slipped off her luxurious fur then headed to the library where was customary to savor a beverage prior to our private rehearsals. On this occasion, however, I would decide which alcohol we would consume rather than allow her freedom of choice. The witch-test required the suspect to drink a full shot of Amaretto in one swallow while wearing the chicken-feather-boa atop a white garment in the presence of a blessed black cat.

In all her lady-like patience and manners, Claire stood aside, waiting for her beverage while I retrieved from the lower doors of the cabinet, a small gift-box fastened with one single white ribbon. Handing it to her, I explained that I made it special for that evening's private rehearsal of Beethoven's Sonata No.9; Op. 47 in A Major, a piece I chose for its difficulty and immense range of emotions which would reveal the precise source of her talent. Her smile betrayed the images of expectation running rampant in her mind. When she opened the box, a long soft sigh slipped between her innocent pink lips, followed by an inculpable smile. She drew the pink feathers across her face, commenting how soft they were, and inhaled the scent of roses which permeated the boa from rose petals I collected from my garden and placed within the box to infuse the cheap fowl feathers.

With the boa wrapped around her neck and shoulders, I poured our glasses of Amaretto and called for Hortico, explaining that I wanted him to share in our toast for what would be a remarkable evening of melodious discovery. Hortico responded to my call, sauntered to and sat in the doorway, staring at both Claire and I while we raised our glasses toward him and drank. Hortico issued no reaction. He witnessed no evidence of witchery through his blessed eyes. He as much as pronounced Claire free from the debauchery of witchcraft.

Without warning, a burst of celebratory, booming laughter rose from my belly, escaping my mouth for a full ten seconds. Claire looked on with confused amusement at my rare exhibition of laughter but took delight when I scooped Hortico into my arms and thanked him for eliminating what would have been an impossible task to achieve without him. In that moment, it became clear that Claire's gift was not of evil witchery, instead, it emanated from somewhere within her body. The witchery test finished, I offered Claire another glass of Amaretto to which she accepted as we sipped in a slow manner before proceeding to the cellar.

Claire opened the first movement teasing its slow 18-bar introduction with seductive mastery. When the A-Major-key shifted to darkness, a piano accompaniment was to couple with the violin. With no piano in the cellar, I would play its section on my Stradivarius, never taking my eyes off of Claire. The aura grew from and transformed around her as we taunted each other — the angry A-minor Presto ensued as Beethoven intended. My natural strength echoed her ferocity with dominance. Our conflict concluded in an anguished coda, leading to the second movement without flaw of transition.

The second movement, Andante con Variazioni, guaranteed to reveal the vestal root of Claire's endowment. During the eighteen-minute movement, five distinct variations transliterate the theme with complex chords and trills to challenge even the most accomplished violinist's expertise. Yet, of course, Claire presented every intended sentiment to one's imagination of small wildlife being chased by an unseen predator through the forest dabbled with shimmering sunlight between lush trees' foliage while birds flittered about chirping an excited warning for other small creatures nearby to scurry to shelter.

The aura surrounding Claire changed colors as a kaleidoscope in furious motion shooting shards of every color, saturation, and depth — excepting the structure from her forearms down to her delicate hands where the ambiance remained constant with a deep, cold, blue-halo wrapped around her arms, vibrating and expanding outward to envelop her entire being while strengthening each syllable of music drawn from her bow. Consistent in its tenacity, I knew this to be the source, the origin, the provenance of her mysterious forte — the secret disclosed as I realized the sinew in her arms were like the strings on a violin. Yet, in her case, she, the instrument, wore the strings inside — protected in a constant environment of controlled temperature, encapsulated in her own, unique rosin.

During the last movement, perspiration beaded upon Claire's face which took on an ethereal glow reflective of her love for the music which ran through her veins, her blood, her tendons. Yes. Her tendons. I would have those sinew. They would stretch upon my Stradivarius and call forth never-before-heard strains of music even the masters could not have imagined.

There was much to prepare over the next two months prior to our symphony's first performance to be held at the Academy of Music in Philadelphia on January 7 in the year 1933. Like a squirrel gathering nuts for winter hibernation, I stocked my supplies for curing and making catgut, unsure the quantity of potassium hydroxide Claire's tendons might require since hers would be unlike anything I have worked with before. I knew how to make catgut from four-legged animal intestines, preferred the Great Horned Owl's above all else, yet had no inclination as to how human tendons may compare in strength or duration upon my Stradivarius. Those concerns were brief compared to planning Claire's demise, for she had to die unstressed, to not sour the blood, still flowing through her veins, with fright as I cut the tendons from her still-living corpse.

With owls, I employed a fail-proof system of an easy death after catching them in my homemade trap baited with live chickens. While the owl feasted on the chickens, the trap would snap shut and I waited until early morning to withdraw him, my arms protected with raptor gloves and a rag soaked with just enough chloroform to render him drowsy — not dead. The magnificent beast lay ragged in my grasp while transporting him to my cellar where I lay him upon a bed of lime, salt, and lye within the glass aquarium to slice its jugular. As the owl bled out in a slow, almost pious manner, I sliced opened its guts, pulled the intestines, scraped off the fat, and transferred the intestines to a jar of water where they would steep for twelve hours. When the owl let loose its last breath, I said a prayer, lifted its body, and submerged it into a drum of sulfuric acid to melt into a liquid abyss.

Although collecting wildlife in this manner was not prohibited, I chose to have the bed of lime, salt, and lye merely for reasons of cleanliness, not to hide an illegal act. Blood is thick, sticky, stains, and can smell, yet, the girth of an owl is less than even Claire's diminutive size, I would need a larger aquarium and to purchase more absorbent.

The night of the deed, I came to Claire's home, knowing she would be alone in the boarding house as all other occupants attended an Orthodox service nearby. Not expecting me, she answered the door with a surprised yet welcoming smile and offered for me to enter the home to which I declined, explaining that she must leave with me immediately, that I needed her help with revising the last movement of my Rhapsodie de Claire Elise which debuts in only two weeks.

Claire, the beautiful, trusting soul that she was, accepted my weak explanation and readied herself to leave, pausing to write a note to Mrs. Grufftune, the boarding house matron, informing her of Claire's whereabouts. I grabbed the note, telling her there was no time, that she would be back before the housemates even knew she had been gone. My musical genius is only rivaled by my ability to lie in such a convincing fashion that sometimes even I believe my lies — part of me began to play the scene in my mind of returning Claire to the boarding house after helping with my composition.

At my home, Claire strode to the library instinctively for our usual drink before proceeding with any business. I touched her elbow, leading her to the cellar, and told her that we would drink while revising the composition.

In the cellar, Claire sat in one of the twin leather rough-hewed chairs while I poured our drinks, Grand Marnier with Regan's Orange No. 6 bitters. The bitters I added to her drink would hide the rancid taste of Laudanum, which I did not add to mine.

While playing the last section of Rhapsodie de Claire Elise, I pretended to stumble with the chords, shooting a woesome look toward Claire which begged for her help to smooth out the awkward transition from the angry melody to a finale of gentle peace. Her eyes looked upward, searching the heavens and her narcotized brain for a solution that I knew her incapable of providing for she was an instrument, not a composer. I offered her another drink, this time laced with even more Laudanum which would render her unconscious.

I repeated the last intermezzo over and over until Claire's fluttering eyelids grew heavy, closed and she dropped the empty glass — all toxin consumed. Lifting her to the aquarium, I stripped her clothing and laid her body onto the mixture of lime, salt, and lye. For an extra measure to assure she remain unconscious and free from pain, I doused a cloth with chloroform and held it over her nose and mouth for ten seconds. When I felt assured she was sufficiently anesthetized, I began slicing open the skin on her arms.

After all delicate tendons were stripped, scraped of any muscle and fat, I placed them in the fresh jar of water to steep for twenty-four hours and returned to cutting up the cadaver. While the body parts began disintegrating in the drums of sulfuric acid, I raked the granules of lime, salt, and lye within the aquarium to present a clean, freshly graded calmness to my atmosphere then proceeded to my bed on the upper-most floor, lit the fireplace where I laid Claire's clothes to be consumed by the fire, then pulled shut the heavy draperies for an uninterrupted night's sleep in absolute darkness.

In the morning, I headed to Claire's boarding house and inquired to see her. Mrs. Grufftune explained in an agitated manner that Claire was not there and her whereabouts unknown. I asked her to be certain to let Claire know that I needed to see her post haste, I even wrote a note to Claire which Mrs. Grufftune promised to give to her upon her return. My performance was without equal, had I not been a master violinist, surely I would have been the ultimate actor, accumulating many Academy Award Oscars.

The evening of January 7, 1933, arrived with clear, frozen skies hanging above the concert hall, the glittering stars seemed to applaud my upcoming performance of the long-awaited debut of Rhapsodie de Claire Elise. Conductor Stokowski paced behind the stage voicing his concern for Claire's whereabouts. She had missed three rehearsals. No one had seen her for weeks. Stokowski interrogated me as it was well known that Claire rehearsed privately with me in my home. I projected great concern for her whereabouts but assured him that she would be with the symphony that night, and she would be, but in a different form. She was already there, with me, strung upon my Stradivarius which I anticipated would breathe out her Heavenly talent.

All musicians in place, Stokowski at the helm, the curtains opened to a full house which exploded with applause as I took center stage and began the intro to my magnum opus, Rhapsodic dc Clairc Elise. Every stroke of my bow upon the strings of Claire drew forth even more beauteous sounds than Claire had produced. Throughout the recapitulation and the final refrain, the strings responded to my unspoken desire as though they were alive in some other conscious realm, knowing their purpose.

All these years later, fifty to be exact, never have I restrung my Stradivarius. Claire has been with me through wartime, peacetime, and now, as I lay upon my death bed caressing my violin between weakened arms. My body will be found along with the note I wrote that I am to be buried with my Stradivarius. My headstone would read:

"Here lies Rishley Corvus Corax, musical genius,

with his beloved Stradivarius and Claire,

forevermore."

Author Bio:

Sue Marie St. Lee writes tales that challenge your imagination and poems that touch your heart -- one way or another. She has featured in several international horror anthologies including Black Hare Press releases, of which two are being released in September, "Sloth" and "Ancients". Her poems and prose can be found on Spillwords Press. A short fantasy tale will be published on The Paper Djinn, September 1, 2020. Her most recent work is expected to publish October 7, 2020 in an anthology inspired by Edgar Allan Poe. This latest publication is by invitation only. Beyond this time-frame, many more tales are in progress, including her late son's Memoir.

Forevermore, My Beloved

by Terry Miller

The grandfather clock stood collecting dust, not too surprising as the rest of the house shared in its affinity for the collection. The home long stood vacant, save for myself, atop the ominous cliff which overlooked a foreboding sea beating the sides of the rising earth with monotonous waves rich with resolve. Crippling fatigue bewitched me the day she fell into those menacing waves. What should I care if the home we shared be covered with dust, plagued with webbing, and infested with mice which scurry across the cold, wooden floors at night for their own sustenance? At least something within the walls of this tormentous prison fights for life. Perhaps that is enough to honor her memory!

Many nights I stood where she stood, imagining the stalling of time in the fragmented seconds of her fall; perplexed concerning what thoughts plagued her mind once her decision was made. I contemplated my own descent into the chilling depths but the courage was far from me. How many nights I prayed the cliff would give way, casting the damned house, and myself along with it, to be washed out to wherever the cold waters carried her! What could not be reunited in life could, perhaps, be so in death. Then the grandfather clock would chime, waking me from my illusion that there was anyone listening merciful enough to rid me of my wretched mourning.

Time moved on while life stood still, each day a dreadful repeat of the last, an agonizing realization that my love chose the sea over me. Had I been such a monster? Did I present her with no other choice but to dive into the arms of Death himself? Tell me it isn't so! How I long for one last kiss, one last embrace.

My spirit pleas to be free from this mortal shell and begin upon my own journey to discover any path she may have left for me to follow. How much a fool am I to ponder her effort in reuniting with the man she most loathed, the monster from which she fled! My heart aches for my love and, reluctantly, it beats, for my cowardice condemns me to this incessant suffering. I am damned in this life, what do I fear in death?

****

I recall the first night I saw her ghostly figure beneath the crescent moon, her dress dancing in the wind as if she bore some corporeal form. She stood at the edge of the cliff, gazing over the waters; lost in her thoughts like the night I last saw her beauty in the moonlight. I stared down the neck of an empty bottle as the wind outside blew through an open window. I caught a chill and went to close it. It was then I saw her. I ran in drunken fervor to the door and unsteadily down the steps. Stumbling, I quickly made my way toward her until I fell flat, my face planted in the dirt. I looked up from where I lay only to see the vastness of the sea. She was gone. I fought but the tears mixed with the dirt and all strength to return to the house escaped me.

There, at the edge of the cliff, I slept until the sun of the morning illuminated my face and blinded my opening eyes. In my heart, I felt as though I had twice lost my beloved. As I dawned the door of my home, I heard that wretched bird caw, "Nevermore", as if to purposely mock my longing. I ducked as I saw the black terror charge toward me and fly overhead. It landed on the cliff, it the precise place she had stood, then took off to disappear below the cliff not to be seen again. My loathing for that raven is void of end, yet I thought it peculiar to land where it chose to plant its feet. Perhaps I was mad and imagined her last night, or it was a dream. But that could not explain how I awoke at the cliff lest I have begun to sleepwalk. The truth was unbeknownst to me.

****

Night came and, by the light of a candle, I took to my quill and paper to scribble my thoughts in hopes that, somehow, writing them down would provide them escape from my mind. I thought not of how my sorrow had taken root further than simply my mind or heart, my soul beckoned for release from the chains in which it was held captive. I sought release in bottle after bottle of various spirits which only served to deliver me to the night in a contemplative state of mind.

This time, well haunted by the spirit of a bottle, I heard her. Her sweet voice hummed a song, carried on the wind to my attentive ears. I stood at the door with my shoulder braced against the wood and watched her dress flowing in the night wind. This was not a dream. I walked slowly out to her. I was just feet from her when she turned her head to face me, her smile more intoxicating than any spirit that touched my lips. I reached out to touch her and my hand passed right through. Her form dissipated and her sweet song faded on the wind. I looked down as the waves crashed against the earth. *Coward.* If only I could fly as the raven, I could be so brave.

****

Day after day, I watched her outside my window for hours. The way her dress moved in the breezy night was mesmerizing. Somehow, the raven perched itself upon her shoulder and she would lovingly stroke its feathers. I bore witness to this mystery for a week before I forced myself to stay away from the window altogether. Why was it that the bird could perch upon her, yet my hand passed right through as if she wasn't even there? I feared for my sanity and pondered whether both she and the damned bird were merely illusions.

One night, I found myself particularly exhausted and retired before dusk fell upon the outside. I crept below my cover and listened to the crackling fire in the fireplace as it lulled me to sleep. After a few hours of rest, as chill slithered up my spine; the intensity of it jolting me from my sleep. I stood from the bed and added a log to the fire. It quickly caught flame and I returned to my peaceful bed. A few minutes later, the chill again provoked me to shiver and a ghostly arm slowly moved across my chest. I looked to my left to see her lying there as though she, too, were resting beneath the cover. Terrified, I reached to throw her arm away from me but to no avail. The cover fell and she disappeared from my eyes. I sat up in bed, now wide awake and would be so for the remainder of the day.

***

The morning dragged on and my hand violently shook as I raised my cup of coffee to my lips. It was one thing to see her standing on the edge of the cliff where I was safe behind the wooden door. But now she was visiting me in the place of my slumber like a dream, only I knew full well a dream she was not. All morning since, I suffered the chills climbing from my lower back to my neck, the hairs that met my spine standing on end. I hoped the coffee would warm my bones but even a raging fire did little to do so. I sat in my favorite chair with a cover, listening to the wind off the coast pick up as the morning wore on.

***

When the grandfather clock chimed five times, I was already half a bottle into the only therapy I knew. I moved my chair closer to the fireplace and for a while, the chills left me; perhaps a result of the scotch. I rocked back and forth, wondering how long I could fight the need for sleep. It was yet early, but the occurrences of the night before begged me an early night. I fought but began to doze.

I was out when a knock came to the door. I hesitated, for visitors were rare and their rarity was preferred. The knock came again.

I shuffle toward the door and moved the bolt. Upon opening, I gasped at the visitor before me. There she stood in the dusk, her eyes seeming to peer into my soul. She turned to walk away then stopped to look back at me. Her head nodded as if for me to follow. I did.

We stood at the edge of the cliff, periodically she would turn to gaze into my eyes the way she used to when we first met. Had I been wrong? Had I not been the reason for her choosing death as opposed to her life with me? My mind raced with its confusion. I felt the chill again. Then I felt her hand, solid as yours or mine. It took mine into her own. I was startled as the raven perched itself upon my shoulder, opposite Annabel. It stood, the calmest I ever witnessed it to be. Oddly, I wasn't frightened. The touch of Annabel's hand calmed me the same as it had always done. The three of us stared out across the waves.

She stared again into my eyes, a familiar longing shared between us. The raven, finally, startled me with a word different than the only one I ever knew it to speak.

"Forevermore!" It cawed so loudly in my ear.

Annabel's hand squeezed mine. "Forevermore." She repeated the word to me in a whisper.

"Forevermore!" The raven cawed once again before taking to flight over the waters.

Annabel took a small step toward the edge and pulled on my hand. *Forevermore*, I thought. In death, we could be together forever. Alone, I was a coward, but she had always been my strength. I heard the raven caw once more and we both jumped from the cliff. On the way down, my love again disappeared. The last thing I heard was the bird reminding me of the permanence of my decision with another caw.

"Forevermore!"

Death will own us both, and somewhere, dear Annabel, I will find you—forevermore.

Author Bio:

Terry Miller is an author and poet residing in Portsmouth, Ohio, a small city in the southernmost part of the state bordering the Ohio River. His work has been featured in various publications, print and online, from around the world. He received a nomination for the 2017 Rhysling Award from the Science Fiction and Fantasy Poetry Association which garnered him a spot in their annual Rhysling Anthology for his nominated poem "Salome's New King". He has a split collection, with author Stephen J. Semones, called "MONSTERS" available on Amazon and two short stories for Kindle titled "The Congregation" and "Blaspheme the Digital Messiah". Terry continues to pursue his writing in hopes of writing his first novella within the next few years.

Made in the USA
Columbia, SC
28 July 2024

39400521R00033